I0726890

Shenanigans
SERVING PARANORMALS
SINCE THE DARK AGES

WITCHY
Shenanigans
2

WITCHY SHENANIGANS

PEPPER MCGRAW

CONTENTS

PUBLISHING HISTORY
The Witching Hour | Pure Textuality PR | June 2018

Cover and inside images from Dreamtime:
Witch Legs Broom © Kakigori
Dragon Silhouette © Elena Kozyreva
A Glass of Beer © Leonora Adamchuk

ISBN 978-1-951247-21-8

Edited by J.L. Troughton
PMG Publishing

1

"THEY'RE BACK," MAX announced.

Cole groaned and signaled Phoenix for another beer. He knew exactly what was coming and was pathetically grateful they were having their meeting at the local shifter bar, Shenanigans.

"Someone's gotta do something," Karl said. "We can't have humans just wandering through the woods. They could see anything!"

Max nodded. "Time to step up to the plate, Cole."

"Why me?" Cole demanded, even though he knew exactly what they were going to say.

"Because they're trespassing on cougar, not wolf, territory," Max said, "which means you've been nominated."

"Why not Dan? He's a cougar too!"

"You're crazy if you think I'm going to go talk to some human females about anything," Dan retorted.

"And what's wrong with human females?"

Everyone looked up at the question.

Phoenix stood there, a tray of beers in her hands and an annoyed look on her face.

Cole was relieved he wasn't the one she was glaring at. Phoenix had been raised among humans, so who knew what she'd do with Dan's beer now that he'd gotten her riled up?

Dan shrugged. "I suppose normal human females are okay, but these women – they're not normal."

"And how do you know that?"

Max cleared his throat. "Well, they keep trespassing on our lands while naked."

Phoenix stared at them for a long minute before finally asking, "Are you sure they're not shifters? Because my experience with humans is they're kind of prudish when it comes to nudity. Whereas y'all, meaning you shifters—"

"Uh, you're a shifter too," Dan interjected.

Cole winced. While that might be true, Phoenix had only recently discovered her shifter form and still considered herself to be more human than not, so he wasn't sure Dan's statement was going to help matters at all.

"*You* shifters," Phoenix repeated, raising her voice and ignoring Dan's statement, "tend to get naked at the drop of a hat. And not for any sexy shenanigans either, just for—"

"Oh, we get naked for sexy shenanigans too," Cole assured her.

She rolled her eyes. "Anyway, as I was saying, being naked in the woods tends to be a pretty big indicator of shifterhood."

Max sighed. "But they're not shifting, Phoenix. They smell human and all they do is walk into the woods buck naked, dance around in a circle, pick a few weeds and walk out again. Still naked."

"Interesting," Phoenix said. "Though I'm still not sure why it's a problem, even if it is unusual."

"They could see anything out there, Phoenix," Pete exclaimed. "That's where we shift. That's where the cubs run and play. And now we've got naked humans wandering around who might see something they shouldn't."

Cole sighed. "I'll go and talk to them."

"Excellent!" Max grinned. "Glad that's taken care of."

Cole grunted. Of course the damn wolf was happy. He wasn't the one who'd be dealing with crazy females, and human ones at that.

2

"WHAT HAVE YOU two done now?" Megan stalked inside The House of Light, the store she owned with her two sisters, and glared at them.

Lara and Jessica glanced at each other, then faced Megan together, looks of confused innocence on their faces, not that Megan bought that for a minute.

"What are you talking about, Megan?" Lara asked innocently.

"Oh and I suppose you two idiots have no idea why both Jerry and Steve just hit on me."

"Who're Jerry and Steve?" Jessica looked at Lara, who shrugged and said, "More importantly, are they cute?" Both women turned back to Megan expectantly.

"Cute?" Megan threw up her hands. "Maybe. If you consider ninety-eight-year-old men cute. You know how I know they're ninety-eight? Because they told me so. I learned their entire life stories in the five minutes they detained me outside C's. Steve went on and on about his stamina being great for his almost ten decades on earth and Jerry told me he'd rock my world if I'd only give him a chance. When the two started arguing about who would be a better match for me, I escaped into the store."

"Wait." Lara laughed. "Are you talking about those two old geezers who sit at that picnic table outside the grocery store all day long, chatting and playing chess?"

"Now you're getting it."

"Why, those old coots," Jessica said. "I had no idea they had it in them."

"I'm sure they don't. So why don't you two fess up? What have you been up to? Because it wasn't just Steve and Jerry."

"It wasn't?" Jessica grinned. "Well, come on. Who else was hitting on you?"

"Let's see, Craig Miller – you know, the married owner of C's – hit on me in the frozen foods section and then his daughter Barb asked me out when I was paying for my groceries."

"Isn't Barb engaged?" Lara asked.

"No, that's his other daughter, Natalie. But that's not the point! Why has everyone gone mad? Did you two cast another spell?"

Silence.

Megan stared at her sisters' guilty expressions. "You did, didn't you? What did you do this time?"

"It was only a little spell!" Lara burst out.

"We hardly gave it any power at all," Jessica said. "Just a little push, nothing major."

Megan huffed. "Your nothing major always turns into a disaster. I'd hate to see what you'd accomplish when you're really trying. Now tell me exactly what you did."

"We just burned some herbs and asked for help, that's all," Lara said.

"What herbs and help from whom?"

"Basil, nutmeg, bay leaves." Jessica said.

"Lavender, cinnamon," Lara said.

"Verbena, crocus," Jessica continued.

"Seriously? What'd you guys do? Use every herb associated with love potions?"

"Every one we had or could find." Jessica grinned.

"And that was a lot," Lara said. "Though we might need to replenish some of our stock."

Megan huffed out a breath. "And the help?"

"Eros and Aphrodite," Lara admitted.

"What is wrong with you two?" Megan exploded. "You just threw everything at the universe in the hopes of what? That chaos wouldn't come knocking?"

"Well, actually, we were just hoping for a virile, hot guy," Jessica said.

"Preferably one young enough to wear you out," Lara said. "We weren't exactly going for the nonagenarian set."

"Nona-what?" Jessica asked. "You just made that word up."

"I did not. It means someone who's in their 90s. I think at the very least the universe could have given Megan a sexagenarian."

Jessica laughed. "Yeah. A sexa-something anyway."

"You two are too much. You need to figure out how to reverse that spell and now. I don't have time for a man, even if he is a nonagenarian."

"I think we can do better than Jerry and Steve," Jessica said.

"Definitely," Lara agreed. "Maybe we need more lavender."

"Or elder. We really should have waited for our next order to come in," Jessica said.

"Or maybe not gone casting at all," Megan snapped.

"Oh, that wasn't an option," Lara said. "You're so uptight all the time, Megan. You're constantly working and driving us crazy, wanting us to do the same."

"And there it is," Megan said. "So you didn't even cast a love spell for my benefit."

"Of course it was for your benefit," Jessica said. "We're not the ones in dire need of sex."

"Ahem."

The cleared throat made all three women jump.

Megan whirled and gaped at the man standing just inside their shop door.

Tall and lean, with sandy-brown hair and green eyes, he was the epitome of the virile, hot guy Jessica had mentioned only moments before.

"Well, hello there," Lara said. "Can we help you?"

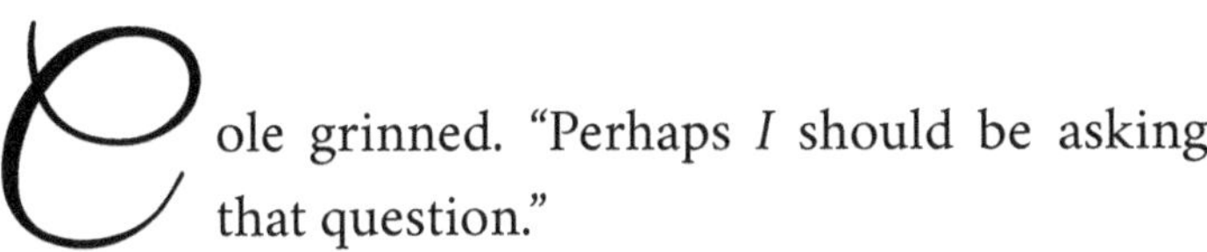

Cole grinned. "Perhaps *I* should be asking that question."

Two of the women laughed, but the third glared daggers at him, even as a blush covered her face and traveled south. He wondered how far that blush went.

Ah, redheads. They were so much fun.

"Was there something you needed?" The angry blusher asked. "Because if not, we're very busy."

Cole made a show of glancing around the shop and then back her way. "Yes," he said dryly. "I can see that."

He didn't think it was possible, but her face turned even redder.

"So," one of the other women spoke brightly. "What brings you into our shop today? Were you looking for a gift, just window shopping or…" She let her words trail away suggestively.

Now Cole was in a quandary. He'd come here for a reason and had even rehearsed what he was going to say on the way over. How to say it without causing offense or suspicion. Now though, every word he'd rehearsed was gone from his head. Which wasn't necessarily a bad thing since accusing someone of trespassing was no way to make friends.

And he and his cat definitely wanted to make friends with these lovely ladies. In fact, the second he'd stepped into the store, his cougar, usually a lazy cat in the afternoons, had stretched and come to attention. His focus hadn't wavered from the three women in front of them since.

Closer, his cat rumbled.

With a sigh, Cole obliged and took a step forward, inhaling deeply. Their scents were different than he expected.

Human, but with something a bit more. A tang or a spice and one scent–

Ours. His cat swiped at the air, trying to catch that scent.

They're human, Cole snapped while fighting to keep claws and fur from sprouting. Stupid cat.

Ours.

Ugh.

The angry blusher made an exasperated sound and muttered something about defective spells as she swept behind the counter.

Great. He was off to a fabulous start.

"Don't mind her," one of the women said. "She's always like that."

"Cranky," the other woman agreed. "I'm Jessica and this is Lara."

Cole grinned and introduced himself, then asked if they were sisters.

"How could you tell?" Lara asked.

Cole laughed. "Just a wild guess." Involving lots of gorgeous red hair and freckles.

Not ours.

Of course they're not. I told you. They're human.

"Lara, Jessica," the woman behind the counter snapped. "We have work to do. If you're not going to help, you might as well just take off. And work on reversing something important."

Ours.

Jeez, his cat was ridiculous today.

Lara and Jessica both grinned.

"But Megan, I think it's working perfectly," Lara said.

"Yes," Jessica agreed, "I'm pretty sure we ordered hot and vir–"

"That's enough!" Megan snapped.

Megan, Cole's cat rumbled. *Closer.*

Cole obliged, moving across the room toward the counter where Megan was pretending to work. At least he thought she was pretending.

Ours. His cougar was now pressing against his skin, trying to get as close to Megan as possible, trying to savor her scent, which Cole had to admit was intoxicating, a fine layer of sweet with an undercurrent of spice, unlike anything he'd ever encountered.

He waited, hoping to get a glimpse of her eyes again, to see if maybe he was wrong and there was an animal lurking somewhere inside, but she just kept her head down, shuffling things in the case, refusing to look at him.

"So you're Megan?"

She grunted.

"I'm Cole." He leaned against the counter and inhaled.

Human. Definitely human.

Ours, his cat rumbled again.

Okay, okay. Fine.

"So," Cole drawled out the word, trying to remember his plan. What was he supposed to be asking again? Something about trespassing. And naked dancing. He couldn't believe he'd missed seeing that!

Megan darted a glance at him, enough for him to see that she was perfectly human. Not a hint of an animal anywhere in her gaze.

Disappointing.

"If you don't need anything–" she began.

"A date," Cole blurted. "I-I mean, I was wondering if you'd like to go out sometime. To dinner."

Her hands stilled on a piece of jewelry, but only

for a moment. If he hadn't been watching her so closely, he would have missed it.

"I'm busy."

Cole laughed. "I haven't suggested a time yet, so–"

"I'm *always* bus–"

"That sounds great!" Lara startled him as she bounded up and hooked arms with him.

He'd completely forgotten the other two women were there, his attention had been so focused on Megan.

"She'd love to go out with you. How about tonight?" As Lara spoke, she turned them toward the door and started to walk him out.

"Lara!" Megan exclaimed behind them.

"You can pick her up at seven," Lara said cheerfully. "Does that work?"

"Um. Yeah, sure."

"Great!" Lara pulled open the door and practically shoved him out.

"All right, so I'll see you tonight, Megan!" Cole called as the door shut in his face.

"What is wrong with you?" Lara whirled around and glared at Megan.

"Me?" Megan exclaimed. That was just like Lara, acting like someone else was to blame, when the entire fiasco was clearly her fault. "What about you? What do you mean telling him yes?"

"Well, someone had to do something!" Lara exclaimed. "Otherwise, you were going to let all that sexiness just walk out the door. What a waste of our time!"

"And herbs!" Jessica agreed.

Megan threw her arms up in the air. "No one asked you to go love-casting and I certainly didn't give you permission to use up all our herbs on such a fruitless quest!"

"The herbs belong to all of us," Jessica said. "Just like this shop and the land out back. You don't get to make all the decisions just because you're the oldest."

"Oh, really?" Megan said dryly. "From what I can tell, you two are the only ones making decisions around here and ones that directly affect *me* and no one else."

Jessica and Lara glanced at each other, then back at Megan.

"Okay, valid point," Jessica said, "but we did it for your own good."

Megan glared. "Oh don't give me that good-for-me crap. I don't need a man to make me happy."

"Of course you don't," Lara said soothingly. "But wouldn't sex be nice, at least every once in a while?"

"That's what batteries are for."

Jessica blanched and Lara giggled.

"I really didn't need to know that," Jessica muttered.

"Well, at least she's taking care of some of the stress," Lara said. "Otherwise, she might have exploded by now and not in a good way."

Megan rolled her eyes. "Whatever. One of you can go on that date tonight because–"

"Oh, no," Jessica said. "He didn't ask us out. He asked you."

"Because of your stupid spell," Megan exploded. "What were you thinking? I don't want a man who's only interested in me because of some stupid spell you two cast!" She shook her head. "What am I saying? I don't want a man at all, but definitely not one under those circumstances."

"Oh, but we were really careful," Lara said.

"Yeah, we cast the spell specifically for your true mate."

"And how does that explain Jerry and Steve? Or Craig and Barb?"

They both shrugged.

"Feedback?" Lara suggested.

Megan groaned. "You two are crazy. I'll go on this date, but only because it would be rude not to. But I'm not fancying myself up and I'm not shaving!"

Lara's eyes widened and she tossed a panicked glance at Jessica.

"Close the shop," Jessica ordered. "This is an emergency."

3

"A DATE!" PETE let out a hoot of laughter. "I thought you were going to talk to them about trespassing!"

Cole shrugged. He hadn't exactly gotten around to that conversation.

"Did you find out why they were dancing in the woods?" Pete asked.

"Not really. I mean, they were talking about herbs for spells when I walked in so–"

"Spells? You mean like witches and magic?" Karl asked.

"I'm not sure." Cole had no intention of telling them he was pretty certain Lara and Jessica had set a sex spell on their sister, Megan.

Good thing he didn't believe in magic. Otherwise, he'd think the spell was the reason his cougar was all riled up.

"Is that why they were naked in our woods?" Dan asked.

"We didn't exactly get around to talking about the dancing naked part."

"What? That was the whole point, Cole!" Max exclaimed. "You were supposed to get them to stop trespassing."

"Yeah, well, that's the problem."

"What?" Max asked.

"My cougar's convinced she's his mate, so he doesn't think of it as trespassing. In fact, my cougar likes that she's been on his territory."

Max groaned. "Well, is your cougar right?"

Cole shrugged. No way was he admitting that he'd been about to talk to her about the trespassing when he'd blurted out a request for a date instead.

Yeah.

Either she was his mate or the sex magic thing had really worked.

He definitely preferred the mate theory.

4

*H*OW DID SHE get into these situations?

Megan sat across from Cole at the one steak-house in town. "I'm a vegetarian, you know."

Cole looked horrified. "Seriously? You don't eat any meat at all?"

"None."

"But, but that–that's just wrong!"

"Wrong?" She'd never had that reaction before. Sure, some people didn't understand her choice, but to call it wrong?

"Well, I mean, um–don't you ever get the urge for a juicy hamburger? Or a steak? Or–" Cole broke off and glanced around, a worried look on his face.

"Should we go somewhere else? I'm not sure they'll have anything for you to eat."

Megan laughed. "I'll be fine. They've got a salad bar and lots of sides."

"Yeah, but I'm not sure the vegetables won't be contaminated. I mean they might cook them on the same grill with the meats."

Megan smiled, charmed in spite of herself. "I'm not that vigilant. Yes, I choose not to eat meat, but I don't expect others to make the same choice, and I refuse to worry about a little cross-contamination when eating out." She shrugged. "Now Lara, she's a whole different level. She's a militant vegan and let me tell you, shopping can be a real challenge when she's along, especially in a small town like this one."

"I bet."

~

Cole was completely charmed.

At first, he'd been sure his cougar had gone mad. After all, Megan was human and not at all what he'd envisioned for their mate. Even worse, she was a vegetarian, a fact that had shaken even his cougar. However, as the night wore on, he realized how perfect she really was.

Told you. His cat stretched lazily, smug satisfaction in every movement.

Yeah, yeah. I still think a vegetarian human is a little much, but I'm on board.

Beyond her sense of humor, which turned out to be a great match for his own, Megan's favorite activity was hiking in the woods. *His* woods. That was really what convinced him.

Anyone who loved his woods as much as he did was okay in his book.

Cole was already planning their second date. He'd take her to his favorite waterfall. Maybe if things went really well, he'd even show her his cougar. Thinking of the woods reminded him of why he'd walked into the shop in the first place, which reminded him of the conversation he'd overheard when he first went inside.

"So did I understand your sisters right? Were they talking about casting spells?"

Megan blushed. "They seem to think I need help getting a date. So they cast a love spell. I'm pretty sure it's the only reason you asked me out, but I won't hold it against you."

Cole laughed. "I assure you, I didn't ask you out because of some spell."

"You say that now, but you're not the first person

to ask me out today."

"Really." Cole and his cougar were not pleased to hear this.

"Yeah. My sisters are either the best or the worst spell-casters in the world. I'm not really sure which. I don't think any of us are."

"Right." Cole had no idea what to think. Was she joking? Was she serious? Her sisters didn't really believe in magic, did they? "So how does that work? I mean, is it a religious choice, like are they Wiccan?"

"I suppose there are some similarities, but really we're just witches."

"Wait. You too?"

"Of course."

"But you don't believe in magic." Cole was convinced his mate couldn't possibly believe in anything so ridiculous. Then he saw the look on her face. "I mean. Right?"

"Of course I believe in magic. Don't you?"

"Well, ah. Not exactly. I mean–"

"But you're a shifter. How can you not believe in magic?"

"Wait. How'd you figure that out?"

She shrugged. "My magic recognizes yours. What are you, a cat?"

Cole's cougar preened. "Not just any cat, darlin'. I'm a cougar." He was also freaking out. How did she know about shifters? She was human! "What do you mean your magic recognizes mine? I don't have any magic."

"Of course, you do. All living forms have magic, but shifters have an even greater share, almost as great as witches."

"Oh, come on," Cole scoffed. "Next you'll be telling me your sisters really *did* cast a love spell."

"Of course, they did. It's why we're here right now. Their spell brought you to me and compelled you to ask me out."

"That's ridiculous. No one compels me to do anything and besides, there's no such thing as magic."

~

Megan gaped at Cole. How could he not believe in magic? He had a giant cat inside him!

"I don't get it. I mean, you're a grown woman and you actually think you're a witch?"

Megan laughed. "And you're a grown man who thinks he's a shifter."

"Yeah, but I can prove that. We can go out in the woods right now and I'll shift for you."

Unbelievable. He actually thought she wouldn't be able to prove magic existed. "You do know there are more paranormals in the world than just shifters, right?"

Cole shrugged. "Sure. Um. Well."

Megan rolled her eyes. "You've never met another paranormal, have you?"

"Of course I have! I've met bears."

"Those are shifters."

"And wolves."

"Also shifters."

"I even met a koala."

"Still a shifter."

Cole huffed. "Well sure, but–"

"There are all kinds of paranormals in the world, Cole. You shifters aren't the only ones out there. You just like to stay in your forests and caves and bury your heads in the sand about the rest of us. Well, we're here – the Djinn, the fae *and* the witches – and whether you want to believe it or not, we're all quite steeped in magic."

"And I suppose you've met a Djinn before, have you?"

"Well, not a Djinn, but–"

"That's what I thought."

"Hey, just because I haven't met them doesn't mean they don't exist!"

"Sure and just because your sisters cast a love-spell doesn't mean they actually have magical powers."

5

"AND THEN HE told me I shouldn't rely on magic to get me dates because I was just lucky he happened to stop in the store at the right time. Otherwise, I probably would have been waiting forever!"

"He did not!" Lara exclaimed.

"Oh, yes, he did! And then he tried to backtrack, saying his words came out wrong, but I think they came out just fine!"

"Well, that's rather disappointing," Jessica said. "I had high hopes for that hottie."

"Me too," Lara said. "I hope you told him off!"

"Oh, trust me. He definitely felt the bite of my tongue."

~

"Cougar Boy!" Max let out a bark of laughter.

Cole scowled. He hadn't meant to let that bit of information slip. He was just so incredulous. He couldn't believe how quickly she'd taken offense, especially considering most people didn't believe in magic.

"So they actually think they're witches?" Karl asked.

"Yep. And they also believe in genies and fairies," Cole said.

"I knew a Djinn once." Glory, one of the owners of Shenanigans, paused on her way by. "He was a lot of fun."

Max scowled. "And where would you have met a Djinn?"

"You do know I had an entire life before moving to Jamesville, right?" Glory shook her head and stalked off.

"Man, when are you going to just ask her out and be done with it?" Pete taunted Max with a grin.

"I don't know," Cole said. "I mean, she *is* a black bear. I'm not sure Max has what it takes to handle a raging she-bear."

"I think we need some cheering up," Lara said. "Sure our first candidate turned out to be a dud, but I know where we can find some other paranormals to flirt with."

"Oh, no," Megan said. "Count me out."

"But it's a Shenanigans, Megan," Lara said.

"Really? There's a Shenanigans all the way out here?" Jessica asked.

"Yeah, it's in the woods, pretty far off the beaten path."

"Well, I'd be willing to bet it caters exclusively to shifters, considering Cole's never met any of our kind and doesn't actually believe we exist," Megan said.

"Shifters," Jessica muttered. "So isolationist."

"So does that mean the women really *are* witches?" Pete asked.

"What are you talking about?" Cole shook his head in disgust.

"Well, if Glory's met a genie, then witches might exist too, right?"

"My dad used to tell me stories of the Djinn," Max said. "He'd never met one, but always said there were probably more paranormals out in the world than we shifters knew about. He never mentioned witches though. And even if they do exist, I seriously doubt they'd smell human like our trespassers. My guess? The women are completely normal humans."

Cole scoffed. "They're anything but normal, Max."

"Well, all right, I'll grant you that. Let's just say their *ab*normal isn't exactly *para*normal."

Glory, who'd been walking by with another tray of beers, stopped dead right behind Max, then shook her head and walked on.

She definitely knew something they didn't and Cole expected her to return at any moment to educate them.

Sure enough, after delivering a couple beers to a table of wolves, Glory wandered back their way. She grabbed a chair from a neighboring table and shoved her way in between Max and Pete.

Cole grinned. This should be fun. A cranky black bear in between two idiotic wolves.

"So. What are you guys talking about tonight?"

Max gave her a suspicious glare. "Why?"

"Well, first I hear you chatting about the Djinn

and then about witches. So now I'm curious. Has Jamesville finally expanded beyond shifter world? Are we actually getting more paranormals in our humble town? Do share."

"You know that witches don't exist, right?" Cole said.

"Really? Who told you that?"

Cole glanced around the table, but everyone else just shrugged. Fine. If they wouldn't say it, he would. "Common sense."

Glory laughed. "Okay, so did common sense also tell you that humans can't shift into animals?"

"We're not humans," Karl protested.

"You sure do look human."

"Knock it off, Glory," Max said. "Just tell us what you know."

"The Djinn exist. So do witches, the Fae, vampires, even mermaids."

"And you know this exactly how?" Cole asked.

"Do you know what Shenanigans is?"

"Oooh, I know this one," Pete said. "It's a bar."

Glory rolled her eyes.

"An awesome bar." Dan spoke up for the first time. He probably figured someone needed to finesse the situation. "A place where we can relax and enjoy our libation of choice."

Karl groaned. "What is it with you cougars?"

"What?" Dan asked innocently.

"It's not just a bar," Glory said impatiently. "Well, it is, but there are Shenanigans all over the world and you know what every Shenanigans has in common?"

"Oooh, I have a guess," Pete exclaimed. "A black bear bartender?"

Everyone turned and stared at Glory's brother, Travis, who at that moment was kissing the breath out of his mate, Phoenix.

"Jeez. Every night it's the same," Glory grumbled. "I'm happy for Travis, don't get me wrong, but I really don't need to be around my brother when he's feeling frisky. It's just gross. And to answer your question, Pete, no. Not every Shenanigans has black bear owners or bartenders. But they do have *paranormal* owners and bartenders, so that was a pretty good guess."

"Yes!" Pete pumped his fist.

Cole shook his head at Pete's antics. "So what's your point, Glory?"

"My point is that every Shenanigans is open to all paranormals, though many cater to a specific kind. For example, this Shenanigans caters to shifters, mostly because shifters live in the area. But if another kind of paranormal were to walk through that door – *any* kind of paranormal – they'd be welcome. Shenanigans is neutral territory, no matter where it lies."

"How come I didn't know this?" Max demanded.

"Have you ever left Jamesville?"

Max thought about it, then shrugged.

Glory nodded. "I wouldn't be surprised if most shifters have no idea about the Shenanigans network. You know why?"

"Why?" Cole asked.

"Because shifters at heart are isolationists. We burrow in our sleuths, our clans, our packs and we stay there. Even when we wander, we do it in such a way that we avoid those not of our sleuth or clan or pack."

"What about humans?" Dan asked.

"What about them?"

"Well, are they allowed in Shenanigans? Because I'm pretty certain three impostor-witches just walked in the door."

6

THE MOMENT THEY walked into Shenanigans, Megan knew she'd called it correctly. The air inside the bar felt furry, which of course was ridiculous, but she didn't know how else to describe it.

Her magic bristled.

"Do you feel that?" Jessica asked.

"How could I not?" Megan muttered.

"It's like a shifter paradise in here." Lara stared around the room as if she didn't know where to look first.

The bar was mostly filled with men, though there were a few women as well. Despite all of them being in human form, there was no mistaking the preda- tory, animalistic vibe inside the bar. And everyone was staring at Megan and her sisters. Had none of them been around witches before?

"Hey there. Welcome to Shenanigans." A waitress approached with a friendly smile. She had brown hair and brown eyes and at first Megan thought she was completely human, but as the woman got closer, Megan could feel little bits of fur like static electricity pinging off her magic. Definitely a shifter, though not of a kind Megan had ever met before. She glanced at her sisters and saw they had equally puzzled looks on their faces.

"I'm Phoenix," the waitress said.

"I'm Megan. These are my sisters, Lara and Jessica."

"I'm super excited you're here. I've heard all about you three from my mate, Travis." Phoenix must have read the look on Megan's face because she laughed. "Oh, you'll get used to it. These shifters are terrible at keeping secrets." She leaned forward and whispered, "They're such gossips and the wolves are the worst of the lot." She grinned. "See, Cole mentioned he'd met his mate, so of course, all the wolves wanted to know everything and then they gossiped to Travis and he told me."

"Wait. What?" Megan stared at Phoenix.

"Okay," Lara exclaimed. "Can we sit anywhere?"

"Of course. Anywhere you'd like. Can I bring you some drinks to start off?"

"Do you have any Witches' Brew?" Jessica asked.

"I don't know. Let me ask Travis." Phoenix turned and headed for the bar.

"Come on," Jessica grabbed Megan's arm and pulled her to a table.

Megan wasn't exactly happy where they ended up. "Do we have to sit in the literal center of the room?"

"Yes, Megan. Yes, we do." Lara plopped down in one of the chairs and looked up at Megan expectantly.

Megan huffed and yanked out a chair. As soon as they were all seated, she pinned her sisters with a glare. "What was that waitress talking about?"

"What do you mean?" Lara asked innocently.

Megan growled. "You know exactly what I mean." She leaned forward and hissed, "She said Cole met his mate! Are you telling me that mangy cougar took me out when he already has a mate?"

Jessica and Lara just stared at her.

Megan shook her head in horror. "You are kidding me! Your damn spell made that cougar think *I'm* his mate? Have you two gone mad? Why would you screw with people's lives like this? You need to fix this now!"

Jessica turned to Lara and asked, "Has she always been this stupid?"

Lara sighed. "I don't think so. I think meeting her mate turned her brain to mush."

"That cougar is not my true mate!"

"But, Megan, we cast the spell for specifically that. For your true mate to come calling. And he did. Plus he's telling others you're *his* mate so I'm thinking our spell worked."

"In a massive way," Jessica agreed.

"You two suck."

"Guess what?" Phoenix slid into the fourth chair at their table and beaming at them, handed out three mugs with steam rolling off the top. "Travis said he's been hanging onto this bottle of Witches' Brew for seven years, hoping one day he'd be able to serve it." She held up a black bottle that might be close to empty, but probably wasn't. That was the thing with Witches' Brew. You never knew exactly how much of the precious liquid you'd be getting. "I didn't even know such a thing existed or that witches were real. This has been a total adventure for me. So. Question. Will Witches' Brew harm a shifter?"

"What? No, of course not," Jessica said. "It just might be more potent for non-witches to drink."

"More potent?" An incredibly good-looking man grabbed a chair and shoved his way into the group, sitting between Lara and Jessica at the table. "This I have to try." He turned and held out his hand to Lara. "Hey, I'm Dan."

"Nice to meet you. I'm Lara."

They shook hands and then he turned and repeated the process with Jessica. He faced Megan last and said with a perfectly straight face, "So you're Cole's witchy mate."

Megan just gave him a look, then grabbed her brew and took a big gulp. It burned all the way down, in the best of ways.

"What are we having to drink?" Cole shoved his way into the empty space between Megan and Phoenix.

Before anyone could answer, four more hulking shifters showed up, dragging another table in their wake.

Without a word, Lara stood and shifted her chair to the side, so that they could join the two tables. Introductions flew.

Megan caught names on the fly, but wasn't sure she'd remember them all later.

"So what's up?" one of the newcomers asked. Max, Megan thought his name was.

"We're about to taste test some Witches' Brew," Phoenix said. "But we need more mugs if you guys are going to join us." She glanced at the bottle in her hand. "Or maybe shot glasses since I think this is Travis' only bottle."

Megan snickered. "Don't worry about it. I think one bottle will be plenty."

"Oh, honey, if you think one bottle's going to do it, you're just plain mad," Dan said with a grin.

The bartender approached with a tray of mugs in his hands.

Phoenix stood and accepted the tray. "Thanks, honey."

He leaned down and kissed her, then with a grin, said, "Don't get too drunk on that brew, darlin'. It's potent, especially for shifters."

Cole snorted. "Give me a break. It's called Witches' Brew. How bad can it be?"

Megan rolled her eyes and took another drink. If he was going to sit here and pretend he hadn't insulted her the last time they'd seen each other, more power to him, but she wasn't going to engage. He was a jerk and she was ignoring him.

Phoenix handed out mugs to all the men and

then stared at the bottle in her hand, obviously unsure about what to do or how to divide the bottle that appeared to hold a finite amount of liquid between what now counted as seven shifters, including herself.

Megan stood. "Here." She held out a hand. "I'll serve this round."

Phoenix gave her a grateful smile. "Thanks!"

Megan grinned and turning back to the table picked up her own mug, refilled it, then topped off Lara's and Jessica's, before slowly making her way around the table, filling every mug. She began with Phoenix and ended with Cole, hoping that the infamous Witches' Brew would have finally reached the end of its generosity by then, but it wasn't to be. Really, it was too much to hope that a single bottle of Witch's Brew would serve anything less than thirty full mugs, considering its hefty price tag.

She filled Cole's mug too, then settled back in her seat.

The entire table was silent.

She glanced up and the first thing she saw were the grins on her sisters' faces. She took a breath for control, then glanced around the table.

Everyone was staring at the bottle she'd set in front of her with wide eyes.

"How'd you do that?" one of the shifters asked. "And can you do that with any bottle? Like if I order a bottle of The Beast Within, can you make it last like that?"

Megan bit her lip to keep from laughing in his face.

~

"Are you serious, Pete?" Cole demanded. "Are you really thinking that was some kind of spell she cast? It was just an illusion or something. This mug is probably still empty." He lifted his mug and glared at it, certain Megan was laughing at the lot of them.

Jessica grinned from across the table at him. "Well, if you think it's an empty mug, then you won't have any trouble at all chugging it."

Cole growled. "I have no desire to drink air."

Pete, not being anywhere near as discerning as Cole, lifted his own mug. "Well I want to know if the illusion tastes good or not, so I'm trying it." And with a quick glance around the table, he took a huge gulp. Seconds later, his eyes bulged and watered and he began gasping for air. "Damn," he coughed out the word, pounding his fist on the table. "What the hell's in this stuff?" He took another huge gulp, eyes wide as he swallowed it down, then gasped and choked some more. "It's damn good," he rasped.

Cole rolled his eyes. That idiot wolf had no damn sense at all, though his reaction to the Witches' Brew did make Cole a little leery to try it now. And considering what Travis has said to Phoenix, maybe Dan was wrong and one bottle *would* be enough.

Cole glanced at Megan out of the corner of his eye and noticed she'd almost completely finished her own mug of the stuff. She also didn't seem at all affected the way Pete was.

Damn lightweight wolf. Making shifters look bad in front of the humans.

At that moment, Pete leapt to his feet. "Jenny!" He raced around the table and met his mate as she walked toward them. He swept her into his arms and kissed her. After a few moments of that – long enough for Cole to wonder if Pete would actually come back or if he'd just hustle his mate out the door and back to their den – he led her to their table, saying to her as he arrived, "I'm so glad you made it."

"Hey, Jenny," Cole said and the others echoed his greeting.

Pete grabbed a chair for her and everyone shuffled a little to make more room.

Travis brought another mug so Pete grabbed the bottle of Witches' Brew and everyone watched with wide eyes as he filled the mug for Jenny. Pete then introduced her to Megan, Lara and Jessica.

"I've never met a witch before," Jenny said to them. "I was so excited when Pete told me. I made him promise to text me if you guys showed up here."

Megan smiled. "It's really nice to meet you, Jenny."

"Thanks. So what's it like being a witch?"

Cole rolled his eyes. Seriously. He glared at Pete. Like he needed someone encouraging Megan's ridiculous beliefs.

Pete just shrugged, clearly unconcerned that Jenny was making the situation worse. If that was what it was like to have a mate – to lose all common sense – Cole wasn't sure he was on board after all. What if Phoenix was right and he ended up believing in witches and magic and other absurdities? He shook his head. That wasn't even possible. He was entirely too sensible for that.

"So how do you guys know you're witches?" Dan's voice brought Cole's attention back to the table. He realized he'd missed whatever answer the women had given Jenny, but that was okay because Dan's question was about a thousand times more reasonable.

"What do you mean?" Lara asked.

Jessica rolled her eyes. "He doesn't really believe we're witches, Lara." She glared to Dan. "We were born that way, idiot. Just like you were born with a furry half."

"Yeah, but how do you know? I mean I can shift, that's how I know, but how do you know you're a witch?"

"We cast spells," Lara said. Though she wasn't as outspoken as her sister, her voice still implied she thought Dan was a moron.

"Yeah, but when you cast spells, how do you know if they work? I mean, what if they don't work? How do you know if you're any good or not?"

"Oh, they're not any good," Megan assured him. "I'm great at spell-casting, but they're both terrible."

"Cut it out, Megan," Jessica said. "We're all fabulous at our craft."

"Yeah," Lara agreed. "It's just some of us are a little more uptight than others." She gave Megan a pointed look.

"So can you prove it?" Cole asked abruptly.

Megan slowly turned to face him. "Prove what?"

"That you're witches. That you can - you know – do magic. Like, can you cast a spell or something else to prove your powers?"

"We're not trained pets you know," Megan snapped. "We don't perform on command."

"Oh, come on." Pete leaned forward. "We'd love to see you cast a spell, even a small one."

"Oh, yes, please," Jenny said with a happy smile.

Any minute now, she'd start clapping, Cole thought sourly.

"Are you kidding?" Dan asked what Cole was thinking. "I mean, you don't actually believe they're going to cast a spell, do you? There's no such thing as magic, Pete. I'm sorry, Jenny, but there just isn't. And even if witches did exist, I guarantee these three humans don't have the tiniest bit of magic in them."

Dan was sitting right beside Jessica which meant everyone's eyes were on the two of them when it happened.

She flicked her fingers and Dan yelped and disappeared from sight as his chair collapsed beneath him.

The table was frozen for just a second then Dan popped to his feet and stared wide-eyed at Jessica.

She smirked at him.

Cole growled. "Don't be ridiculous," he snapped at Dan. "She had nothing to do with that."

Dan huffed and grabbed a new chair. He pushed the remnants of his old one to the side and gingerly sat down, all the while eyeing Jessica suspiciously.

Megan sighed. "Jeez. We can't take you anywhere, Jessica."

7

MEGAN WALKED THROUGH the woods with her sisters, super conscious of the two drunken cougars slinking through the shadows in their wake. Did they seriously think she didn't know they were there? She was a witch for heaven's sake, one of the most powerful of their generation, and her sisters weren't bad either.

"We should cast a spell on them," Jessica muttered drunkenly. It was pretty obvious she was still fuming over Dan's comments earlier.

Megan smirked. Maybe their love spell had backfired and Jessica would be the one to find her true mate. Still, casting a quick spell wasn't a bad idea. Megan pulled energy from the earth and spun it around them, obscuring their forms and muffling their voices.

Lara glanced around, nodded at Megan, then asked Jessica, "Hey, how'd you know his chair was going to collapse like that?"

"I didn't." Jessica grinned. "I had condensation on my fingers and was flicking it off. It was just bad timing."

Lara laughed. "Or really great timing! Did you see the look on his face?"

"You know they're going to keep harassing us to prove we can cast spells," Jessica said.

Megan shrugged. "Let them." She took a pull straight from the bottle of Witches' Brew. Best money they'd ever spent since it showed no signs of emptying out anytime soon. "We don't have to prove anything."

Jessica reached for the bottle and drank deep. "True, but it might be kind of funny trying to convince them."

"Ooh!" Lara jumped up and down. "This could be so much fun! Imagine the havoc we could wreak and all with their permission."

Megan shook her head. "Okay, well, you two have fun with that. Me, I'm not jumping through hoops for anyone."

"We wouldn't be jumping through hoops. We'd be *choosing* to cast certain spells with the goal of freaking them out!" Lara grinned.

Megan rolled her eyes. There was no way this wasn't going to get out of hand fast.

8

THE NEXT MORNING, Megan looked up when the door to the shop opened.

Harry, the owner of the one hotel in town, wandered in. He'd never been in their store before. Actually most of the town residents had never visited, which was fine with the sisters. They did most of their business online anyway.

He glanced around, eyes skimming past crystals of varying power, dreamcatchers, tapestries with embedded protection wards and other objects of the light, before landing on Megan and lighting up.

Great.

He made a beeline for where she stood behind the counter. "Hey, Megan." He beamed at her.

"Hi, Harry." They'd met when the sisters had first

rolled into town. Their great-aunt's shop and upstairs apartment had needed a lot of work before they could move in, so the three sisters had stayed at the hotel for a very long three weeks. Harry was super nice, but not the greatest hotelier, considering his was rundown in the worst of ways. Megan was kind of shocked it hadn't been condemned yet. "What can I help you with?"

"Well, see." He shuffled his feet. "I was kind of hoping maybe you might like to go out sometime. You know, for dinner or something."

Megan could feel her smile freezing on her face. Damn her sisters. "Um, Harry, I'm so flattered, thank you, but I'm already seeing someone."

"Oh." His face fell. "Okay, then, well, thanks anyway." He turned to go.

"Oh, wait."

He turned back eagerly.

"I have something for you. Hold on a second." She hurried around the counter to the shelves of crystals by the door. She was pretty sure it was on these shelves. She scanned them, searching for the small crystal she'd seen. It didn't have much power, so wouldn't work on paranormals of any kind, but maybe for someone like Harry, whose wishes would be simple and whose heart was pure—there! Grabbing the tiny blue crystal, she carried it back to Harry. "It's not a guarantee or anything, but this crystal might help. There's someone out there perfect for you, Harry, and this crystal may just be the boost you need to attract her into your life."

He stared at it, brow wrinkled. "What do I do with it?"

"Just carry it in your pocket with your loose change. It might work right away. It might never work. But it's worth a chance, right?"

"How much?"

Megan shook her head and reaching out, took his hand and placed it in the center of his palm. "On the house." She curled his fingers around the crystal. "In thanks for your hospitality when we first arrived."

He stared at his hand, then looked at Megan, a stunned expression on his face. He cleared his throat. "Um. Thanks."

She smiled. "You're welcome, Harry. And thank you."

He nodded briskly and walked out the door, the crystal clutched in his hand the entire way.

"That was really nice," Lara said at her side.

Megan shook her head. "He's a nice man and your spell messed with his head."

Lara sighed. "I know. We didn't take into account

the number of humans who would be vulnerable to suggestion. But as soon as you're mated, the effects will wear off and everything will go back to normal."

Megan groaned. "Seriously? That could be never, Lara!" She stormed around the counter.

"Don't be silly," Jessica admonished from the other side of the room. "The spell's already working. You just have to be open to the arrival of your true mate."

"I already tried that," Megan snapped, "and the asshole I opened up to called me crazy and hard-up to boot!"

"He didn't say that," Lara said.

"Close enough!"

~

Cole arrived in time to catch the door from closing as Harry walked out, a stunned look on his face. "You okay, Harry?"

Harry stared at Cole a minute, almost like he didn't even see him, then muttered, "I hope it works."

"You hope what works?"

But Harry didn't answer, just turned and strode away, head down, staring at something in his hand as he walked down the street, headed back toward his hotel.

Cole shrugged and went to enter the store, then froze when he realized Megan was talking about him. He winced at her interpretation of his words the day before.

Jeez, he'd screwed up bad.

He'd realized at the bar the night before that his cougar wanted his true mate, even if she *was* crazy and thought she was a witch. She and her sisters had drunk all the wolves under the table and only Dan and Cole had been upright by the end of the evening.

Travis had had to carry Phoenix upstairs because she'd curled up in a corner booth after barely half a mug of their Witches' Brew.

The wolves had passed out all over the bar and Travis had just rolled his eyes and told them to sleep it off. The cougars he'd set out after the sisters, to ensure they made it home safely. Cole had barely restrained his cougar from mauling that stupid bear. As if he needed to be instructed to care for his own mate.

Of course, halfway between the bar and the town, that crazy fog had rolled in and they hadn't been able to see the women or even hear or scent them anymore, which should have been impossible given their heightened cougar senses. Dan had wondered drunkenly if they really were witches, but Cole refused to believe it. It was just the crazy weather playing tricks on them.

When his cougar had become agitated at not being able to follow their mate and had insisted they travel to her home anyway to see if she'd arrived safely, Cole had realized he had no choice but to fix things between him and Megan. Now, hearing the hurt in her voice, he knew he'd have to do a lot more than just fix things. At the very least, he'd have to apologize and mean it.

~

When the door opened for the second time that morning, Megan tensed, expecting yet another human wanting a date to enter.

Instead, it was the cat.

She scowled at him and turned away.

From the corner of her eye, she saw Lara and Jessica make a beeline for him. Good. Maybe they'd get rid of him.

"Megan."

Megan stiffened and turned around just in time

to see the door to the shop closing behind her sisters. The traitors! They hadn't sent him away, but instead had hurried out themselves, leaving her all alone with the asshole. "What do you want?"

"I wanted to apologize."

Megan huffed. Like that was going to make a difference.

"And I was hoping maybe you'd like to go on a hike with me."

Megan stared at him. Was he seriously asking her out on another date? Even though she thought it was sweet he'd remembered her favorite hobby was hiking, she had no intention of going down that road again. "Not a chance. I'm not going out with someone who won't even accept me for who I am!"

"Aw, come on, Megan, give me another chance. I won't let you down, I promise."

She glared at him, but then remembered how Lara had insisted he was her true mate and how Jessica had said she needed to be open to the possibility. If her sisters were right, turning him down might mean turning her back on her one true mate— not that she needed a man, but if he was meant to be hers— "Fine," she said curtly.

Cole grinned. "Awesome! I have the most amazing place to show you."

An hour later, Megan stood at the base of a small waterfall, thrilled at its pounding glory. "It's incredible."

Cole grinned. "I'm glad you like it. This is my favorite place in all our territory. I wanted to share it with you. You're welcome here any time."

It was a true place of power. She wondered if Cole understood how much power thundered through the river and the earth and from the top of this waterfall to its base. She wondered if he understood how much power he exchanged with the earth on a daily basis.

She shook her head.

Probably not. He was a shifter. Simple in his thinking. Certain he was the only being of power on the earth.

"What are you thinking right now?"

She didn't even hesitate. "That this is a place of power. I've only been here a minute and my magic stores have been filled to the brim."

She felt more than saw him stiffen at her side. Great. He might be her mate, and a cougar, but in reality, he was a stubborn goat.

Cole cleared his throat. "I'm sorry, Megan. I–I know I wasn't very accepting before. I just didn't expect you to claim to be a witch. I've never met a witch before. So I was taken off guard."

Megan sighed. Maybe she shouldn't be so hard on him. Shifters were an isolated lot, kept to their own kind. If he'd never met a witch before, it wasn't hard to understand why he disbelieved.

"Um, do you think maybe–I know you didn't want to last night, but, I mean, would you be willing to show me a spell or something? I promise to keep an open mind."

Though she'd taken offense the night before, not wanting to perform on command, in the light of day it seemed the simplest solution. She'd show him something basic, but with enough power to truly convince him, and then they could move past this and maybe discover whether he truly was her mate, or whether it was just the influence of her sisters' spell.

9

"YOU'RE HERE EARLY," Travis said as he set a beer in front of Cole.

"Needed a drink." He grabbed the beer and chugged it, trying not to think about how everything had ended with Megan.

"What's wrong?" Travis leaned on the bar and waited.

Cole shrugged. He didn't feel like he should say anything. It felt disrespectful and somehow wrong to share his mate's shortcomings with others.

"Another beer for my man here, and one for me too, please." Dan slid up to the bar and settled beside Cole.

"You got it."

"So lay it on me, Cole." Dan turned to face him.

"What's got you looking like you lost your favorite kitten?"

Cole shrugged. He wasn't going to say a thing. Not one word.

Travis set a beer and a shot glass in front of Cole. "Enjoy."

An endless number of beers and several shots later, Cole was thoroughly drunk. Sadly, all the drinking had accomplished was to make him even more depressed. The more he drank, the more he thought about Megan and the more depressed he became.

And so he drank some more.

It was a never-ending cycle of pain

And while he'd been drinking his way down that cycle, the bar had been filling up.

Dan stood, grabbed both their beers, and said, "Come on," then led the way to the wolves.

This was a brilliant idea. Why hadn't he thought of the wolves before? They could definitely help solve his problem.

"Of course we can help solve your problem!" Pete exclaimed cheerfully.

Had he said that out loud?

"Just tell us what's wrong and we'll get to the solving."

Dan rolled his eyes. "I've been trying to get him to spill his guts for three hours."

Had it only been three hours? It felt like days had passed since the disastrous second date.

"You went on a second date?" Max asked.

Damn, Cole was drunker than he thought if he was spilling his guts to the wolves without even realizing it.

"I assume it was with Megan, the little pretend witch," Max said.

Cole nodded morosely. "My mate."

"So what's wrong?" Pete asked. "How come the date was disastrous?"

"My mate's crazy." Cole enunciated his words very carefully, wanting to make sure the wolves understood he wasn't exaggerating or making stuff up. "Like really crazy."

"Which one's your mate?" Cole looked up at Phoenix, who stood at their table handing out beers.

"The pretty one," Cole said.

Dan laughed. "They're all pretty, dude."

"Megan."

"She didn't seem crazy to me," Phoenix said. "Actually none of them seemed crazy at all."

"Well, trust me," Cole said. "They're all crazy, but especially Megan."

"How do you know?"

"She thinks she can do magic!" Cole flung out his arms, causing Dan and Max on either side to jerk back to avoid being hit in the face. "Isn't that enough?"

Phoenix rolled her eyes. "This again? Really? If I can believe in shifters, why can't you believe in witches?"

Cole looked at Dan and shook his head. Why didn't she understand? "Uh, Phoenix, you're a shifter too. And you've seen us shift. Plus you've shifted. At least once that we know of. So it's kind of obvious that shifters exist. But none of us have seen any proof that witches are a real thing." He nodded emphatically, then shook his head. "Yes, shifters. No, witches."

"Yeah, but didn't one of the sisters make Dan's chair collapse?" Phoenix asked.

"That was just coincidence," Cole said. "Just because the chair collapsed while they were at the table doesn't mean they actually caused it. Or maybe it does. Maybe they sabotaged the chair before Dan sat in it. Did you ever think of that?"

"Okay," Phoenix said. "If you say so." She walked off.

Max sighed. "She doesn't get it. But come on,

Cole. You knew yesterday your mate believed she was a witch and you still went over there today to ask her out. So what's changed? Why are you so upset?"

Cole let out a huge sigh. "I asked her to show me some magic so she did a spell thing. Or at least she tried to and she said it worked, but it didn't. She's just crazy. She was seeing things that weren't there or I guess *not* seeing things that *were* there."

"Did you understand that at all?" Karl asked the rest of the table.

Everyone shook their heads.

"Try again, Cole," Max ordered.

"She did this thing with her hands." He waved his hands drunkenly in front of his body. "And then she just looked at me like I should see something, but I didn't. So I kind of shrugged at her and she told me she was invisible. Invisible, guys! I'm staring *right at her* and she's claiming to be invisible. So I tell her, 'No you're not. I can see you just fine.' And she holds out her arm and looks at it and then looks at me and says, 'Yes, I am. I can't see me and neither can you.' But I'm staring right at her!"

Dead silence.

Then Pete finally said, "Okay, you're right. She's crazy."

"How's your cougar feel about this?" Karl asked. "I mean is he willing to let her go, now that you know she's crazy?"

Cole groaned. "He's depressed, but no, he's not giving up. Even when I tell him she's a crazy human, all he ever says back is, 'Ours.'"

"Wait. Your cougar talks to you?" Pete asked.

"Well, yeah. Doesn't your wolf?"

Pete looked around at the other wolves, who all shook their heads no.

Cole looked at Dan, who nodded and said, "My cat's quite chatty sometimes."

"Huh," Max said. "I would have thought it'd be the other way around. You know, what with cats being so standoffish."

"Well." Cole looked at Dan, who laughed and made a waving motion for him to proceed. "Cougars tend to be argumentative. They're not just going to go along for the sake of going along. Usually when my cougar has something to say, it's because he wants to argue with me. Like this whole witch situation."

"Your cougar believes her?" Dan asked incredulously.

"Of course not. He just wants me to pretend to believe, so that we can have our mate. But I'm not lying to her. I can't."

"Yeah, that's a problem," Karl said.

"We need a plan," Dan announced.

Max groaned. "Not another plan."

"What kind of plan?" Cole asked.

"Well, if you're not walking away from your mate and you don't want to lie to her, somehow you have to get her to admit she's not a witch."

"How in the world am I supposed to do that? I'm telling you, she believed, truly believed she was invisible! Besides, if I keep trying to convince her, she's going to end up hating me."

"No problem," Dan said. "You concentrate on romancing her during the day and we'll concentrate on forcing her to face the truth at night."

"How?"

"By asking the women to prove they have magic over and over again. Every time they fail, we'll explain it's because they're not witches. Eventually they'll realize the truth and then you can have a happy mating."

Max looked doubtful, which was pretty much how Cole felt. "I'm not sure–"

"This'll work," Dan assured him. "You just focus on being her supportive mate. We'll be the bad guys."

"This is gonna be a hoot," Karl enthused. "Too

bad it probably won't take very long since there's no way they'll actually succeed at casting spells."

"I don't know," Cole said. "I bet it takes a lot longer than you guys think it will."

Pete's eye lit up. "That's a great idea!"

"What is?" Cole asked suspiciously.

"A betting pool! We haven't had one of those since we were betting on Phoenix's shifter form."

"Yeah, and look how great that turned out," Cole grouched. "Most of the money went to the bar since no one won half the bets."

"I don't think you should be complaining since you're the only one of us who did win that day," Karl said.

Cole rolled his eyes. "Okay, true. But the point is you guys might lose a lot of money on this betting pool because I bet the women won't ever admit they're not witches."

"What are you guys talking about?" Glory asked.

Cole hadn't even noticed her walking up.

"We're wanting to set up another betting pool," Pete told her. "Will the bar hold our money again?"

"Sure, but the bar's taking a cut."

"Yeah, yeah."

"So what are we betting on?"

"How long it'll take us to convince the humans they're not witches."

Glory froze, then slowly turned her head to stare at Cole. "Seriously? This is the best you can do?"

"What?"

"Why don't you just talk to your mate?"

"I did and she tried to convince me she was invisible!"

Glory just stared at him. "And how'd that turn out?"

"Well, since I could see her the entire time, not so great."

Glory nodded. "I see. So that's your evidence?"

Cole looked at the other men.

Dan jumped to his defense, "Sounds pretty good to me. I mean, if Cole says he could see her, then…" he trailed off under Glory's glare.

After a moment, she relented and nodded. "Very well. I'll hold your money. Set up the board." She waved a hand at the chalkboard on the other side of the bar and walked away.

Thirty minutes later, the entire group had moved to the chalkboard where Max was writing down their bets and collecting their money.

"This is going to be great," Pete exclaimed. "It won't be like last time when none of us guessed

Phoenix's shifter form. This time, someone's gonna win that money, guaranteed."

"It'll probably be me," Phoenix said as she walked by.

"No way, Phoenix!" Pete hollered after her. "We've got this one all wrapped up."

Phoenix laughed and a few moments later, stopped on her way back to the bar. "I've got a new bet for the board, okay?"

Everyone groaned.

"Not again, Phoenix!" Karl glared. "There's no such thing as a never bet."

Phoenix grinned. "While that *is* a tempting bet, I'd rather have added to the board 'the men admit the humans are witches.' I'll put fifty on that one." She slapped down a stack of bills.

Pete whirled toward Max. "Write it down, Max. That'll be the easiest money we ever made."

"You know you're gonna lose that bet, right?" Cole said to Phoenix.

"Not a chance." She shook her head. "Besides, even if I do, I feel like I need to stand in solidarity with my fellow humans."

"But you're a shifter," Pete protested.

Phoenix shrugged. "Raised human. Human at heart."

Max groaned and Cole rolled his eyes.

"Whatever," Pete said.

"Your bet's on the board," Max said. "You can go away now."

Phoenix laughed and wandered off.

10

MEGAN PACED BACK and forth in front of her sisters, ranting. "I just don't understand what happened. How could he see me? It's not that he didn't believe me this time. It's that he *literally* could see me, but how could he when even *I* couldn't see myself? I mean I could, but I could also see the spell lying on top of my skin and clothes, making me invisible. How did this happen? Now he *really* thinks I'm crazy!"

Lara grinned. "So now you care what he thinks?"

"Of course I care, especially if you're right and he's my true mate."

"So you're admitting to the possibility?" Jessica asked.

Megan rolled her eyes. "It's not likely, but I'm not

ruling it out yet. Though maybe I should since he's now convinced I'm completely off my rocker."

"Well, we'll just have to keep trying," Jessica said.

"Keep trying what?"

"To convince them we're witches, of course," Lara exclaimed.

"And how are we going to do that?"

"Stick to the plan," Jessica ordered. "We're going to convince those stubborn wolves and cougars that witches exist and we're three of the best."

~

It wasn't a bad plan, in theory, Megan later conceded. In practice, though, it was one hundred percent flawed.

Cole showed up at their store every day to spend time with Megan. Sometimes they went to breakfast at the diner where Phoenix also worked and sometimes he brought a picnic lunch and they hiked to their waterfall to eat there. During those times, he deliberately didn't ask questions about her magic and she didn't offer any more demonstrations.

Instead, they focused on getting to know each other, though Megan fretted their entire romance was a doomed experiment since she was deliberately leaving out anything to do with magic and spell-casting, both of which represented the majority of who she was. Even worse, the more time she spent with Cole, the more she *wanted* him to be her true mate.

Megan tried desperately not to think about the spell her sisters had cast and how all of this – his feelings for her, his desire to be with her and to get to know her and even his willingness to ignore, at least during the day, what he considered to be her crazy, witchy ways – might be doomed to die as soon as the spell wore off.

They lived in a bubble during the day, pursuing their romance as if the worries that plagued them both didn't exist.

And they didn't.

Especially not when Cole spent hours kissing her breathless and making her entire body ache with desire.

Nor when he held her hand as they wandered through the woods.

Nor when he kissed her so sweetly behind the waterfall's curtain, the droplets of water sizzling against her hot and aching flesh.

And certainly not when he trusted her enough to show her his cougar for the first time and they played in the shallows of the river, chasing and splashing each other for hours before collapsing on the banks to nap together, her head cushioned on the soft pelt of his side.

Day after day, she became more and more enamored of him, more convinced than ever that he truly was meant for her. That everything would work out because there was no way it couldn't, not when his every breath, every touch, every kiss made her feel as if she might burst into flames at any moment. Not when his sweet, playful, caring nature had her heart aching with love.

This was what she knew during those endless, beautiful days – they were *meant* for each other.

But then evening always came and with it the quest to convince the bullheaded wolves and cougars that magic was real.

Megan was starting to dread the evenings at Shenanigans, for every time they failed, she worried she was wrong about her romance with Cole. She worried it was nothing but a false construct, held in place only by the power of her sisters' spell.

Though Cole never said anything, just let his buddies do the talking, Megan could sense his disappointment. She couldn't decide if he was disappointed because of her sisters' failure to convince his friends or because of his *friends'* failure to convince them. She was afraid it was the latter.

Then Lara noticed the shifters' betting board and things got a lot more intense. Suddenly, her sisters were tossing spells around like magic was going out of style and things were getting seriously out of hand.

First, Travis discovered all his bottles of scotch were filled with water. He'd stomped over and lectured the women about messing with his livelihood. Lara had laughed, but Jessica had apologized and solemnly waved a hand, restoring the scotch.

Of course, all his bottles were open at that point, which meant he refused to sell any other drinks but scotch for five nights in a row, which got all the wolves and cougars riled up. And of course, they blamed the sisters.

The weirdest part, though, was the wolves' and cougars' refusal to believe the sisters had used magic to switch out the liquids.

"You have to stop sneaking into this bar and causing problems," Dan lectured Jessica.

Jessica glared at him and snapped, "I've never sneaked anywhere in my life, you snake."

She then tried to cast a spell on him, but something happened to the magic and it ping-ponged around the room, knocking over beer bottles and collapsing chairs before zipping back to Jessica and leaving her silent for the rest of the night.

"I don't know what happened," she admitted to Megan later. "I cast a simple silencing spell on him. It should have made him unable to speak for an hour at most. Instead my magic just created some havoc and then silenced *me* for more than four hours!"

"Something weird's definitely going on," Lara agreed.

"Maybe we should stop using our magic until we figure it out," Megan said.

"No way," Jessica said. "I'm going to convince that stupid cougar if it's the last thing I do."

Of course, Megan was starting to worry that might actually be a possibility. She was beginning to see that her sisters were as stubborn as those cougars and wolves.

The next night, Lara's simple levitation spell, something they'd all mastered around the age of three, collapsed the table they were sitting at, something she told her sisters happened *against* the will of her magic. She wasn't even upset at the men's insistence the collapse was caused by a loose bolt because she was so unnerved by the feel of her magic's rebellion.

This was becoming the most disturbing thing about their inability to prove their casting skills to the men. Their magic just wasn't acting as it should.

Even worse, on the few occasions their castings (or the castings of others) worked perfectly – the never-ending bottle of Witches' Brew, the unexpected snowstorm in the middle of summer, the bar's spray nozzle that went crazy and sprayed everyone sitting at the bar – the men refused to believe magic was the cause. Instead, they had a logical explanation for all of it – illusion, climate change, a malfunctioning trigger.

"I'm starting to think it's that place," Lara said sullenly.

"It can't be Shenanigans," Megan said. "We've been able to cast there."

"Badly!" Lara exclaimed.

"Yes, but sometimes our casting works just fine, and that's not the point anyway. Magic *does* work inside the bar. It's just–"

"Warped?" Lara asked.

Megan growled. "It doesn't matter that the magic warps sometimes. It's still magic! The problem's that–"

"The cougars and wolves are too damn stubborn to recognize magic when they see it?" Jessica asked.

Megan pointed her way. "Exactly." Bad enough their magic went a little crazy inside the bar – and Megan had a theory about that – but for the men to not even believe what they were seeing was magic, even after everything they'd witnessed, was entirely too frustrating.

"We need a new plan," Lara said.

"Yeah," Jessica agreed. "Our current one sucks."

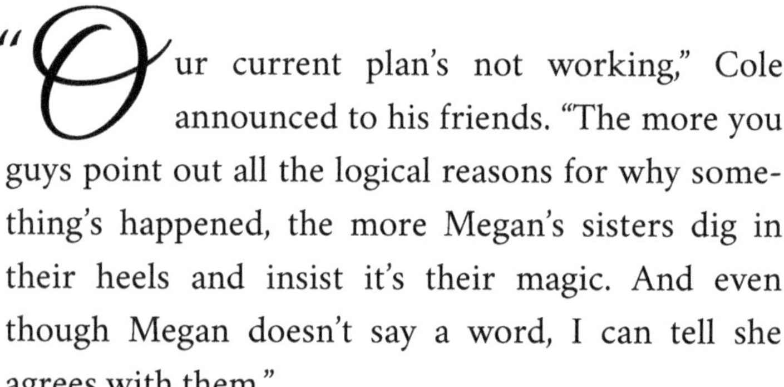

"Our current plan's not working," Cole announced to his friends. "The more you guys point out all the logical reasons for why something's happened, the more Megan's sisters dig in their heels and insist it's their magic. And even though Megan doesn't say a word, I can tell she agrees with them."

Pete chuckled. "Yeah, they're all pretty stubborn."

"I just don't understand why they're so insistent. It's like they've been brainwashed." Cole was at his wit's end. "And my cougar no longer cares. He's just impatient to claim his mate. As far as he's concerned, she can be as crazy as she wants as long as she accepts us."

Karl snorted. "That sounds about right."

"Yeah," Dan said. "I don't know a single shifter who's reasonable about his or her mate."

"What are you talking about?" Travis called from the bar. "I'm perfectly reasonable about Phoenix. And so's my bear."

Phoenix, who happened to be walking by at the moment, stopped, turned and stared at Travis, then looked at the wolves and cougars at the table.

As one, they all burst into laughter.

Travis scowled.

With a huge grin, Dan reached out, grabbed Phoenix's hand and with a jerk sent her tumbling into his lap.

Phoenix shrieked on the way down and then froze and stared at Dan, horrified.

A huge roar echoed through the building and Travis lunged over the bar, claws and fur sprouting as he raced toward them.

Dan hastily set Phoenix back onto her feet and scrambled around the table so that it was between him and a raging Travis.

Phoenix leapt toward Travis and wrapped her arms around his neck, which Cole couldn't help but notice was suddenly much thicker than usual, and her legs around his waist.

Cole shook his head, amazed at Dan's idiocy.

Stupid cougar almost made the bartender go full-on bear.

They couldn't hear what Phoenix was saying to Travis, but whatever it was, he slowly relaxed and his claws retracted, though his eyes still shone with a predator's light and were intently fixed on Dan's crazy face.

Travis growled at Dan, then turned and stalked away, taking Phoenix with him behind the bar where he continued making drinks, carrying her plastered to him from bottle to bottle.

Dan cleared his throat and slowly walked back around the table to his seat.

Pete laughed nervously. "Yes, he's perfectly reasonable about his mate."

"You're an idiot," Cole said to Dan.

"I know," Dan said. "I thought it'd be funny, but really it was quite terrifying."

Cole grinned and then chuckled a little. "Well, it was kind of funny. I mean I've never seen that bear move so fast."

"Or Dan," Max said dryly.

Everyone laughed.

"Yes, yes, quite funny." Glory stopped at their table and glared at them, hands on hips. "Because it's always a good idea to rile up our black bear bartender."

Dan held his hands up in surrender. "Learned my lesson. Won't be doing that again."

"None of this is helping Cole," Karl said. "What do you think he should do, Glory?"

Cole glared at Karl. He didn't need Glory's insane input. She actually believed his mate was a witch. Or at least she was pretending to believe. He wasn't sure which it was.

"What's the problem now?" Glory asked.

"The humans still insist they're witches, even though they have yet to prove they can cast spells," Karl said.

"Or wield magic," Dan said.

"Or whatever else witches are supposed to be able to do," Pete said.

Glory just stared at them. "Maybe you should let the women know exactly what you *would* accept as proof of magic since it seems to me they've managed to show you quite a few things already."

"Like what?" Cole asked.

"How about Karl's hair?"

Everyone turned and stared at Karl whose hair had been purple since Tuesday.

Karl huffed. "That wasn't magic!"

"Yeah, a bucket of paint spilled all over him," Pete said.

"And where exactly did that paint come from?" Glory asked. "Because I've been asking around and literally no one remembers bringing purple paint into the bar."

"That's my point," Cole said. "It's almost like they're running a scam."

Dan's eyes flared. "That's it! Like they sneaked in and loosened the bolts on a bunch of chairs and tables and now they're just randomly collapsing. We should probably all check our chairs before sitting from now on. Or even better, we should switch chairs with the women when they're not looking."

Cole growled. "They might get hurt. They're only human."

"So it's okay for them to do it to us, but not the other way around?" Dan glared at Cole.

Cole bared his fangs.

"Fine," Dan huffed. "But it makes sense! I bet they also set up the paint and it was just bad luck that Karl was the one who got it in the face."

"And where'd the can go?" Glory asked.

"Huh?" Cole asked. "What can?"

"The one the paint came from. The paint appeared out of thin air, dumped all over Karl, then nothing. No container or can or bucket could be found. Just paint."

"They sneaked it back out again, I guess," Dan said.

"How do you explain the floor?" Glory asked.

"What floor?" Max said.

"Paint comes spilling out of thin air, coats Karl and only Karl and not a drop falls on the floor?"

Everyone turned and stared at the spot where Karl had been painted purple.

"They must have cleaned it all up," Dan said stubbornly.

Glory shook her head. "It's really hard to convince people who refuse to see the truth. What you're going to have to decide, Cole, is whether or not your own perception of reality is more important than your relationship with your mate." And with that, she walked away, leaving silence in her wake.

Shit, was she right? Was he just being stubborn, refusing to admit even the possibility that his mate was magic?

"I think this pretty much proves my conclusion," Dan said. "We need a new plan."

"I'm thinking it's not the bar," Megan said. "It's the shifters."

"Yes, their attitude," Jessica agreed.

"Not just that. My magic tingles all the time when I'm around them." Megan raised an eyebrow at her sisters and they both nodded.

"Mine too," Lara said.

"And mine," Jessica agreed.

"That's what I figured. I'm thinking maybe our magic doesn't work on shifters, at least not the way we expect it to. Think about it. When you made the hose go haywire, you had no trouble controlling your magic, right, Jessica?"

"Yeah, that's true."

"And Lara, when you made the paint explode all over Karl's head–"

"He deserved it," Lara said hotly. "The way he kept mocking us, saying our little illusion tricks weren't fooling anyone."

"I know," Megan said. "I'm not saying he didn't. What I'm saying is, you were able to pull a paint can from the shop and manifest it into the bar without any trouble at all."

"Yeah, but that's simple magic, barely takes any energy at all," Lara said.

"Sure, but you weren't directly casting a spell at a shifter. Instead, you were casting it at the air right above his head."

"I don't understand."

"What spell were you casting when the table collapsed?"

Lara blushed. "I told you. I was just trying to levitate it."

"I know that's what you *said* you were doing, but that doesn't make any sense. Not with what I've figured out. So come on. What was the *real* spell you were casting?"

"I just figured the easiest way to convince them was to take control of one of them."

"Oh, Lara, you didn't." Megan sighed.

"It was only going to be a tiny bit of control and nothing he didn't want to do already."

"Who'd you try to control?" Jessica asked.

"Cole."

Megan's eyes narrowed. She couldn't believe her sister had tried to control *her* mate!

Great.

Now she was getting possessive of a man who refused to accept that magic was real.

"I don't get it," Jessica said. "How did taking control of Cole make the table collapse?"

"I don't know," Lara wailed. "It shouldn't have been that difficult since I was trying to make him do something he already wanted to do."

Megan rolled her eyes. "And what exactly was that? And how would you know what he wants to do?"

"He's your true mate, isn't he? I mean, of course he wants to kiss you. Probably all the time."

"And everywhere," Jessica said dryly.

Megan blushed, then realized what Lara had just admitted. "Wait a minute. Are you saying you tried to force Cole to kiss me?"

"It wouldn't have been force, Megan. Not when he wants to kiss you anyway."

"You tried to take away his free will, Lara. That's not cool."

"I know. I just get tired of them acting like we're crazy. It's time for them to admit we're powerful even if we are human."

"I get it, I really do." Megan sighed. "The problem is we're not *that* powerful when it comes to casting spells on *them*."

"What do you mean?" Jessica asked.

"Before you made the paint appear, Lara, what spell did you originally cast?"

Lara shrugged. "I tried to turn Karl's hair purple.

You know, with a simple color cast, but it's almost like the spell bounced off him and–"

"Turned on you?" Megan asked.

Lara nodded and fingered a strand of purple hair. "Yeah, which just made me angrier, especially when he laughed and sneered at me. So I pulled the paint from the house instead."

"And there you go."

"Wait. So you're saying I was able to color his hair by casting a paint can into the air above his head, but I couldn't actually cast his head itself."

"Exactly. I'm thinking the buzz we feel when we're around them is some kind of shifter defense mechanism against our magic."

"Then how was Cole able to see you when you were invisible?" Jessica asked. "You didn't cast blindness on him, but invisibility on yourself."

"Damn." Megan had completely forgotten about that spell. "I don't know."

"I do," Lara exclaimed. "It's because he's your true mate! I've been researching the bond, especially when it happens between a witch and a shifter, and it turns out shifters can see past any glamour their true mates cast on themselves. That's all an invisibility spell is – a glamour that lays on the skin."

Megan rolled her eyes. "I suppose you think this is more evidence he's my true mate."

Lara and Jessica glanced at each other, then nodded.

"You know it could be your stupid spell," Megan said, "making him *think* he's my mate."

"Yes," Jessica said dryly. "Because just thinking that would help him see past your veil of invisibility."

"It could!" Megan said defensively.

"Whatever," Jessica said. "Regardless, I think you're onto something here. And now that I understand what's been really going on, I have a brilliant plan to prove magic is real once and for all. This time they won't be able to ignore the evidence."

11

MEGAN WALKED INTO Shenanigans that night full of trepidation.

Jessica had refused to share the details of her plan, though Megan had later seen her and Lara huddled together speaking in hushed whispers.

Megan was pretty sure the two of them were plotting something she wouldn't approve of, which meant this night could be crazier than all of the previous nights combined, and that was a whole new level of crazy.

"Hey, baby," Cole walked up and slid a hand behind her neck, leaned down and caught her lips in a searing kiss.

"Hi," she whispered when he pulled away.

He grinned at her. "Ready to run away from this crazy place yet?"

Megan rolled her eyes. "Like you'd ever leave."

He laughed and said, "Come on." He pulled her over to where the cougars and wolves were sitting and ushered her into an empty chair, then settled at her side.

Jessica and Lara took the empty seats left, which put them both on the opposite side of the table from Megan and several seats down from each other.

"So, got any new tricks to show off?" Dan raised an eyebrow at Jessica, looking smug and superior as always.

Jessica looked like she wanted to claw his eyes out. "I have plenty of tricks up my sleeve," she told him, "and if you were smart, you'd be wary of inciting the full power of my rage."

Pete let out a hoot of laughter. "Careful, Dan, you're riling the beast!"

Dan growled at him, "Don't be an idiot. She doesn't have a beast, not like mine anyway, and her little parlor tricks have no bite."

Jessica clenched her fists and Megan knew she was grappling for control.

Megan cleared her throat and Jessica glanced her way, drew in a deep breath and nodded.

"Man, haven't you learned yet, every woman has a beast inside her," Max said.

Dan chuckled. "I suppose that's true, but Jessica here, she's just as sweet as can be." He slung an arm around the back of her chair and whispered something in her ear.

Blood rushed to Jessica's face and Megan couldn't tell if she was angry or if something else was going on.

Damn cougars.

They sure knew how to rile up a woman.

"I think Dan's set his sights for your sister," Cole rasped in her ear, making goosebumps break out along her neck and arms.

Megan nodded, though she wasn't sure Cole was right. If Dan was really interested in Jessica, why on earth was he constantly needling her?

"Foreplay, sweetheart," Cole murmured, planting a kiss in her neck and making her shiver.

Jeez. Talk about foreplay. Cole was a master. He'd been torturing her all week, making her body ache and her breath catch in her throat, with only a few simple touches and whispered thoughts in her ear.

Well, and the occasional, devastatingly hot kiss.

If her sisters didn't manage to convince them

about magic soon, Megan was going to go up in flames. She'd never survive another week of this.

"So we've been thinking," Lara announced. "We've been going about this all wrong."

Megan stiffened. Oh, no. What were they going to do now?

Cole gripped her neck and gently squeezed, his touch both soothing her and making her want, all at the same time.

"Wrong how?" Karl asked, turning toward Lara who sat on his right.

"We've finally realized that our magic is misfiring because of who you lot are."

"What does that mean?" Cole asked.

"It means that shifters are mostly immune to our spell casting," Megan explained.

"Well, of course, they are, honey," Glory stopped at their table and stared at them."Didn't you know that?"

Megan shrugged. "We had no idea. I mean, we've met shifters before, but I guess none of us had ever really tried to cast spells on them." She glanced around at Jessica and Lara and they both shook their heads.

"Not until we got here," Jessica agreed.

"And even though the spells we were trying to

cast were mostly harmless, they've been pinging off you guys and causing havoc," Lara said.

Dan opened his mouth and Megan just knew he was going to say something mocking about their magic, so she said quickly, "So what's the plan?"

As if that was the question they'd been waiting for, both Lara and Jessica stood and stepped away from the table to an open area of the bar about five feet away. They turned to each other and held their hands up, palms facing, but not touching.

"Um, are you guys about to do what I think you are?" Megan asked. "Because I'm not sure inside the bar–"

"You want your mate convinced, don't you?" Lara asked.

Jessica threw the table a wild grin. "Brace yourselves."

"Aw, shit," Megan muttered.

Glory backed away from the table as quickly as she could. "I have no idea what they're about to do, but I'm going to hold your wolves responsible if they destroy my bar." She pointed at Max.

"My wolves?" Max asked. "What about the cougars? It's his mate's sisters!" He pointed at Cole.

"And if you lot weren't so stubborn, this wouldn't be happening at all."

~

Cole ignored Max and Glory. This was typical for them – their bickering was a prolonged form of foreplay that as far as he could tell, might never end.

Instead, Cole was focused on his mates' sisters. He wasn't exactly sure what they were doing, but their red hair was dancing, almost like a wind was lifting it.

A moment later, he became aware that his skin felt as if all its fur was standing on end. He glanced at his arm, almost expecting to see that he'd shifted without knowing it, but it was still human, though as he watched, dark fur rippled and moved, then was gone.

He jerked his head back up and stared at the women. What were they doing? Hadn't they just said they couldn't cast magic on shifters, so how was it they were pulling on his beast?

The air in the bar was still.

Cole glanced around and realized everyone was staring at the two women.

He jerked his gaze back to them and almost missed it. Something swirled around their forms, there and gone so quickly he wasn't sure what he'd seen. And then it happened again and again. It was gray and moved in spirals, a flash of movement toward their heads, then their hips, then at their shoulders, then their feet.

What was that thing?

Megan stood and pulled Cole up with her. She dragged him back from the table a couple steps. "Stay here," she said to him. "I'm going to have to help them control it."

"Control what?"

"Just stay back, okay?"

She walked toward her sisters and made a large circuit around them, just watching.

The spirals moved faster and faster.

Cole was so caught up in watching the spin it took him several minutes to realize what he was seeing.

The gasps of others in the bar told him he wasn't crazy.

The women stood at the center of a tornado. A tiny tornado that whirled around them at ever increasing speeds.

And then the tornado began to expand.

Megan walked faster, her hands dancing in front of her, almost as if she was controlling the movements of the spiral. But how was that possible? How was any of this possible?

There came a loud roaring sound. The roar of the tornado, Cole realized.

It had gotten bigger and was getting dangerously close to his mate.

And then the roar stopped, or actually became muffled, as if the tornado was miles away instead of just across the room.

He stepped forward to go to his mate, but ran into some kind of barrier. He prowled along it, walking at its edge, testing its strength, and made a complete circuit around the women before he accepted he had no way of reaching his mate.

His cougar yowled.

He glanced around wildly and noticed half the patrons had shifted to their animal forms, a visceral reaction to the unnatural weather event before them.

None of the shifters had left the bar though. Instead, they were all riveted to the sight of the tornado that had completely enveloped Lara and Jessica, obscuring the two of them from view.

In fact, the only one of the three sisters they could see was Megan whose hands moved in a whirl as she tried to contain what her sisters had wrought.

12

$\mathcal{M}$EGAN WAS SO furious, she could barely concentrate. She couldn't afford to be angry though. One small mistake and her sisters would be torn apart by the fury of the tornado they'd so recklessly created.

And the minute that happened, she'd lose all control and the bar and its patrons and her mate – her *mate* – would be gone as well.

Damn her sisters.

Dragging more energy from the earth, which was way harder standing inside a building than if they'd done this outside, she cast that energy around the tornado like a thousand lassos and started to pull.

She yanked as hard as she could and the tornado moved.

An inch.

Maybe less.

But it moved.

Slowly, so slowly it felt like eons passed, she dragged the tornado closer and closer. As she pulled it toward her, she also pulled the barrier in so that the tornado's world became smaller and smaller.

She felt the yank and pull when the tornado jerked past where her sisters stood at its center.

She couldn't see her sisters, but she could feel they were all right, though exhausted and perhaps a little terrified.

As they should be.

Dragging more energy from the earth, she yanked the tornado one last time and it swallowed her whole.

~

Cole prowled around the perimeter of the barrier. He couldn't see it, but he could feel it and when it suddenly contracted, he felt that too.

He moved with the barrier, getting closer to his mate with each contraction.

He didn't realize what was happening until it was too late.

Yes, the barrier was contracting, but the tornado was *moving*.

Toward his mate.

Everything happened all at once.

The tornado moved one last time, revealing Lara and Jessica, who looked as if they'd stood at the center of a tornado for weeks. Their hair was insane, a wildly moving tangled mass, and their clothes were full of rips and holes.

They both stumbled and nearly fell, then whirled to face the tornado at their backs, which in that instant, enveloped Megan.

"No!" Cole shouted, hearing Lara and Jessica echo his pain.

❧

*T*he tornado was vast. A wild power her sisters had called from the earth that fought for its freedom.

It was all Megan could do to maintain the barrier between herself and the rest of the bar while also fighting the tornado itself, struggling not to be devoured by its fierce, fiery soul.

She stood at its center and sent soothing energy

into the heart of the storm while slowly siphoning off the worst of its wild fury.

When she had sipped so much of its energy, she felt she might fly apart if she didn't let some of it go, she slowly backed away from where she sensed her sisters stood. She was blind to everything now, just a tornado of energy at her core.

She contracted the barrier so that all it contained was her and the tornado that was her sisters' greatest and worst casting ever and continued to stumble back. She moved on instinct, aware that many forms outside the barrier followed.

She heard a cougar's scream and thought it might be her true mate.

The thought of Cole spurred her on and she kept moving until suddenly she was outside and the whole of the earth was open to her.

~

The tornado that contained Megan disappeared through the front wall of the bar and everyone made a beeline for the door.

The shifters poured out of the bar and froze at the sight before them.

The barrier and tornado had contracted to such a point they appeared to lay over Megan like a second skin. It was as if all three were fused together. As if Megan were the tornado and the barrier, and they were her.

Megan threw back her head, clenched her fists and screamed.

The tornado pulsed one final time, then dropped at an incredible speed, slamming into the earth with such power it flung everyone to the ground.

When Cole looked up, he saw Megan on her knees.

The tornado was gone.

He surged to his feet, stumbled to his mate and caught her up in his arms. He kissed her fiercely, pulled back, then grabbed her and kissed her again. "I'm sorry," he muttered in her ear. "I'm so sorry."

~

Megan clutched at Cole and burrowed into his strong chest. "Why are *you* sorry?"

"For not believing you. For forcing your sisters to cast more and more magic, just to prove what I should have always known. That you were perfect and that I should always believe in you. Your sisters risked their lives and yours because of my idiotic stubbornness."

"That wasn't your fault." Megan pulled back and sent a glare her sisters' way. "They're the ones who should be sorry."

Lara and Jessica were both sitting on the ground a couple feet away, utterly spent from their casting and looking quite subdued.

"What were you thinking?" Dan shouted at Jessica, but she didn't even look up.

He dropped to his knees in front of her and grabbed her up in a hug.

Jessica looked like she might struggle for a minute, but then she relaxed and hugged him back.

Karl settled at Lara's side and slung an arm around her shoulders. "So I guess you really are witches, huh?"

Lara let out a watery laugh. "Yeah, witches who almost killed their sister and everyone in that bar. I thought we'd be able to control it, but–"

"You know what this means, don't you?" Glory asked.

Everyone looked at her.

She grinned. "Phoenix won the betting pool this time."

Travis let out a bark of laughter and Phoenix giggled.

Karl groaned.

"That is so wrong," Pete exclaimed.

Megan shook her head and looked up at Cole. "I just can't even."

He grinned and hugged her hard. "Well, you know our life will never be boring." He laughed. "I'm so damn glad the universe gifted me with you, my love."

Megan made a face. "Yeah, but was it the universe or was it my sisters' out-of-control casting?"

Cole chuckled. "Haven't you figured it out yet?"

"Figured out what?"

"If witches can't cast on shifters…" He raised an eyebrow.

Megan gasped. "Their spell didn't work on you!"

"Not at all. Which means, my dear, that you are really, truly mine."

Megan jumped up and wrapped her arms and legs around Cole and kissed him hard. "And you're all mine." She was almost giddy at the thought. This amazing, crazy, stubborn, ridiculous cougar was her true mate after all.

Keep reading for an excerpt from Max and Glory's
story in FULL MOON SHENANIGANS.

"So when do you plan to claim your mate?" Adam asked.

Max stiffened and glared at his alpha, but Adam didn't react, just waited patiently for an answer.

"When she's ready," Max said grudgingly.

"That's not how it usually works for shifters. You know that, right? I mean, it's highly unusual that she's not ready in the first place."

Max sighed. "She's struggling with the idea of being mated to a wolf."

"Seriously?" Adam scowled. "That's the holdup? Glory's a breedist?"

"No, of course not. She's just concerned because she's so much bigger than me in our shifted forms." Max shrugged. "And in our human ones as well."

"Ah." Adam shook his head. "Such a human hang-up."

"I know, but we do have our human sides, no matter how much we'd like to pretend we don't."

Glory was about four inches taller than his six feet and a good hundred pounds heavier than him. To him, she was the most beautiful woman he'd ever seen and he had the most vivid fantasies about the two of them in bed together, rolling around, wrestling for control, breaking the bed in their enthusiasm.

Adam coughed. "So, yeah. What are you going to do about it? I mean, are you seriously going to wait for her to get over her hang-ups?"

"Of course not. I have a plan for this weekend."

"Uh. You do realize the full moon's on Saturday?"

"Of course I do." Max grinned. "I'm actually counting on it. Glory disappeared last month, but I got Travis to promise to keep her here this time."

"Do you really think the full moon will help?"

"Well, it can't hurt. It should at least level the playing field, maybe help her realize I'm not the puny wolf she seems to think I am."

Adam let out a bark of laughter. "Yeah, no worries about that, especially once you hit the height of moon wildness."

Max waggled his eyebrows. "Here's hoping Glory falls in love with my wild side."

Start reading FULL MOON SHENANIGANS today!

THE SHENANIGANS SERIES

Shifter Shenanigans

Witchy Shenanigans

Full Moon Shenanigans

Hotel Shenanigans

Dragon Shenanigans

Undercover Shenanigans

Spooky Shenanigans

Holiday Shenanigans

Valentine Shenanigans

Lucky Shenanigans

STORIES OF THE VEIL

Guardians of the Veil

Astra

Glory

Luna

Zara

WICKED

No Rest for the Wicked

Wicked Is As Wicked Does

STORIES OF THE VEIL

THE UNVEILED

Astra | Glory

THE VEILED

Luna | Zara

WICKED DUET

WICKED

No Rest for the Wicked | Wicked Is As Wicked Does

ABOUT THE AUTHOR

WWW.PEPPERMCGRAW.COM

PEPPER MCGRAW is a *USA Today* Bestselling Author of paranormal romance. She hasn't met any paranormals to date, but she's sure that moment is just around the corner!

Pepper loves animals, especially cats, and spends her free time volunteering at local shelters and for Trap-Neuter-Release programs.

She's had the supreme honor of winning occasional head butts and meows from the local ferals in her neighborhood and has even convinced a few to come inside and adopt her as their own.

bookbub.com/authors/pepper-mcgraw
facebook.com/ShenanigansSeries
goodreads.com/peppermcgraw
instagram.com/peppermcgraw_author
tiktok.com/@peppermcgraw
twitter.com/peppermcgraw